The Lo.

Adventures of

Marble The Cat

By

Amber Astron Christo

B.Ed Hons; M.A.

Clever Cat Tuition

Amber Astron Media and Music, 2016

wwww.amberastronmediamusic.com

Copyright © Amber Astron Christo, 2016

ISBN: 978-0-9928872-1-6

This book is written in memory of Marble...

CHAPTER 1

THE BEGINNING

Marble was born in Kilburn, North West London. He wasn't called Marble to start with. The boy who owned the mother cat named all of the kittens in the litter, and he named him "William".

He was the most handsome and strong of all his brothers and sisters: with wide stripes across his fur and tan coloured tips to his ears; he would push his smaller siblings out of the way when getting to the food dish. Yes, he liked his food, especially when it was fish, and no one got in the way of that!

As the kittens got bigger, it was decided that they needed to be found new homes to go to. When the twins, Alex and Ruby, came with their Mum to see the kittens, they were quick to make their choice. "Pick me!" William seemed to say, as he pushed his brothers and sisters to the back. "Meow", "Meow", "Meow".

Ruby gathered 'William' up in her arms, his long legs dangling. As Alex opened the cat carrier door, Ruby tried to push William in. It was difficult: he didn't seem to fit! The more Ruby pushed, the more rigid William became, planting his feet firmly outside the carrier and then clawing wildly when he was lifted up. At last, Ruby got William's front feet in. Then, with a final shove, and a sharp slam of the door, he was in! William let out an indignant high pitched "Meow": 'Get me out!' he seemed to say.

The carrier was loaded into the car and they set off to William's new home.

The car stopped. They hadn't gone that far, still in North West London, just a mile or so up the road into West Hampstead, to one of the Greek roads.

"Well, welcome to your new home," said Ruby.

"Yes, and it will soon be welcome to a new name," said Alex. "William is a boy's name, not a cat's, and anyway you're so handsome, you deserve something better!"

"What shall we call him?" asked Ruby.

"Well, look at the pattern on his fur," said Mum. "It really is beautiful, very bold...like a marble pattern...why don't we call him Marble?"

"That's a great name said Ruby.

"I agree," said Alex.

So William became Marble.

Marble was given a cosy basket with a padded cushion to sleep on in the kitchen, but he quickly established that if he crept up to the bedrooms, just after the twins had gone to bed, he could slip onto the covers and snuggle into the feet of either Ruby or Alex. In the morning he would greet them with a "Meow" to say, "Get up, I'm hungry!"

He quickly became part of the family. Apart from the goldfish, he was the only pet and was spoilt rotten. He was allowed to come and go as he chose, through the cat flap in the front door.

He would frequently sit outside by the gate posts, looking up and down the road, like a king surveying his kingdom.

He got to know the familiar sights, sounds and neighbours on the road, (humans and animals). He would see Pat and Cedric from next door most days; as well as Miss Lily who lived a few doors down, (she kept chickens). He would hear the Rock Star playing his keyboards; see the architect working in his office across the road; and watch the children and their friends playing. Marble would also keep an eye on the big black Labrador who would appear sometimes, on his own, sniffing about...

CHAPTER 2

A VISIT TO THE VET

When Marble was six months old he had to go to the vets for his inoculations. Just like children have injections to stop *them* getting nasty diseases, so do cats.

Mr Arkwright the local vet, was very kind. He lifted Marble out of his carrier, talked to him and stroked him to put him at ease. He then proceeded to examine him: he checked Marble's ears and eyes; his leg joints and feet, and finally his tummy.

"What a fine specimen," said Mr Arkwright. "He is a remarkably healthy and strong young cat. I think he will be quite large, as he hasn't finished growing yet."

He quickly prepared the injection, and without further ado, grabbed a handful of skin on the scruff of Marble's neck and plunged the needle in: all done in a few seconds!

"There, not so bad was it?" said Mr Arkwright.

Marble looked slightly dazed; as if he wasn't quite sure what had happened. But he was very brave, and so was Ruby who had bit her lip hard throughout the ordeal. Alex had simply closed his eyes.

Mr Arkwright gave Marble an affectionate stroke before expertly placing him back in his carrier. He turned to Ruby and Alex,

"The injection will stop Marble picking up nasty infections from any stray cats in the area, as well as prevent some common cat diseases."

When they arrived home Ruby and Alex gave Marble a special treat of fishy stew.

"That looks and smells disgusting," said Alex.

"I know, but he loves it," said Ruby, "and he deserves a treat after his first visit to the vet."

CHAPTER 3

ROOF TOP RESCUE!

As Marble grew, he became bolder and ever more inquisitive, wandering up and down the road, and all over the house.

One day, he went out of an open bedroom window onto the roof. It gave him an amazing view of West Hampstead and beyond. He could see for miles...

'I wonder what it's like further down the road?' thought Marble. And while musing over that point in his head, Marble walked across the top of the roof, then jumped down onto a lower section of roof at the back of the house, tiptoed right to the edge and peered over... there was a gap between their house and Pat and Cedric's house, next door. Could he jump? If he went onto their roof, and then walked down the terrace, he could see the view from the rooftops at the bottom of the road.

 'Yes, I can do this' thought Marble. He crouched, gathered himself together and then leapt; like an uncoiled spring he was propelled forward, with legs outstretched. He closed his eyes and when he opened them he had landed on Pat and Cedric's roof!

'Wow! I did it!' He had surprised himself! 'Right, let's explore.'

The next hour or two were spent running from one end of the terrace to the other. He could see Kilburn in one direction, Hampstead in another, Cricklewood and St. John's Wood. London was a *very* big City: so much to explore and see. The fur on his back and tail stood up as he imagined the adventures he could have.

Realising he was getting hungry, Marble thought of going home. But what was that? Oh! That hurt! The sun had been shinning down on the roof top tiles and the hot tiles had burnt the pads on his feet.

Oh! Oh! Each step was very painful. 'Ooh! I can't move. What shall I do?' He meowed and meowed, but no one came. How could they? No one knew where he was.

He would not be able to propel himself back across the gap to the roof on his own house with these feet. He licked his front paws. The pads were swollen, sore and blistered. "Meow...meow." wailed Marble.

Back at home Ruby and Alex had been searching everywhere for the missing cat. Their Mum wrote out notices explaining that Marble was missing and giving a description of the cat. Ruby and Alex took them to the local shops. They also pinned them on trees in the road. It was while they were doing this that they heard a cry, a cat's cry. But, where was it coming from...up there? And then Ruby saw him: Marble was on top of the terrace roof.

"Look, he's up there!" she shouted at Alex, pointing frantically up into the sky. "Look."

"But how did he get up there?" said Alex.

"I don't know, but let's go and tell Mum," answered Ruby.

They ran home, excitably screaming: "Mum, Mum, we've found him!"

Mum came with them, back down the road, and quickly identified where Marble was.

"But how shall we get him down?" Mum said.

"I know," said Alex, "We'll ask Cedric if we can borrow his ladder."

Cedric offered to conduct the rescue himself. Cedric untied his ladder and carried it down the road to the house in the terrace where Marble was now hanging precariously over the edge of the roof, mewing.

 "It's alright," said Cedric. "We'll soon have you down."

Cedric edged his way up the ladder. Ruby covered her eyes, she couldn't bear to look. It was a long way down. Oh no! Every time Cedric got near Marble and went to make a grab, Marble crept back up to the top of the roof. He was now completely out of reach. Despite much encouragement,

Marble would not return to the roof edge again.

"Well, what do we do now? said Mum. "I don't think we have any choice, but to call the fire brigade."

"I agree," said Cedric.

"Yes," said Pat "It's the only way to get him down."

So Mum dialled 999 and in a few minutes not one, but two fire engines drove into the top of the road, all sirens wailing. As the fire engines came to a halt, the fire officers piled out, along with their first female recruit. People opened their windows to see what all the fuss was. Goodness!

"Don't worry, we'll soon have him down" the firemen said kindly to Ruby and Alex.

Marble had come near to the roof edge again, curious at all the commotion. They sent up the female recruit, but when she reached the top of the ladder, and reached out to Marble he simply moved out of reach and went back up to peak of the roof.

"What do I do now?" she called.

"Get on to the roof," said the other fire officers.

"Oh! She won't fall will she?" asked Mum.

"Don't worry, this is good practice, she's a raw recruit," said one of the fire officers.

As she moved up onto the roof, Marble climbed higher, and then disappeared over the top. Oh no, what now?

The house owners came out.

"There's a lower roof in the back garden. Perhaps he'll go there," they said.

Mum went inside the house with them.

"The only way to get to the roof is from the bathroom," they said, and took Mum upstairs.

The small bathroom window was above the lavatory, which made it difficult to get to. But Marble was outside on the lower roof.

"He's there," she called to the others.

She then chivvied Marble towards her. "Meow, meow," Marble responded in a pitiful whine. There was a small gap between the window and the roof. Marble would have to jump.

Standing up on the lavatory seat and pushing her shoulders out through the tiny window Mum called, "Come on Marble jump, jump!"

"Meow....meow," answered Marble.

"Come on," Mum encouraged, "come on..."

Marble crouched, and gathering himself together, leapt forward. Mum reached out and grabbed, pulling him into her arms and then in safely through the window!

Marble mewed. His lips were dry. He was shaking and trembling. Mum thanked the neighbours for their help, and took Marble downstairs. She put him into Alex's arms.

"It's alright," whispered Alex, "you're safe now."

Ruby and Alex took turns to hug Marble.

Back outside, everyone cheered!

"Thank you Cedric! Thank you Fire officers!" said Mum. She turned to the children and Marble, "Now let's get you home."

Marble had a special meal and cold water to ease his parched lips.

He shook and trembled for two days after his rescue, but his pads had healed over within two weeks, and he was soon back to normal. However, something had changed...although Marble still occasionally ventured just outside the bedroom window on to the roof to admire the view, he never EVER wandered further. Nor did he ever jump from home to the roof of Pat and Cedric's house and the terrace of houses beyond.

CHAPTER 4

BATTLES!

Occasionally, Ruby and Alex's little cousin Dan would come for a visit, or even a sleepover, so that his parents could have a baby-free night out.

In his toddler years Dan would chase Marble with glee. Sometimes, if Marble let him catch up, he would pull Marble's tail! "MEOW!" Marble would wail, shaking his tail and winding his claws in and out. He would warn Dan not to repeat the deed, but Dan didn't understand and would time and again yank on Marble's tail. He would pull with all his might, shrieking with delight!

One afternoon, Marble had put up with repeated 'yanks', and had

had enough: he turned to face Dan flicking his tail in anger, wailing and pleading with Dan to stop. But he didn't! The little boy dived again and grabbed the end of Marble's tail and squeezed and pulled at the same time. In a second, just by instinct and because of the pain, Marble swiped with his paw and his extended claws caught Dan just under the eye on his right cheek.

"Oh! Oh!" Now it was Dan's turn to wail...he screamed and yelled 'till his cheeks were bright red, swollen and stained with tears.

"Marble hurt me! Marble hurt me!" he kept saying, shocked that his cat friend had retaliated.

Mum gave Dan a cuddle, wiped his face and put some antiseptic cream on the scratch to prevent any infection. After a bowl of fruit and ice cream with chocolate sprinkles on top Dan soon forgot his injury. By the time his parents were ready to take him home, he and Marble were friends again.

But, to this day, Dan still has a small scar on his cheek: a permanent reminder of his toddler years and a visit to his cousins' house when he tested the patience of Marble, their pet cat.

But, most of Marble's battles were with non-humans. He got a bit of a reputation on the road for being The Boss! The black Labrador, who lived at the bottom of the road, was always sent packing by Marble when he came sniffing around the bins, (the same with the foxes). Occasionally, a really scraggy, thin fox would try to poke the lid off the bin at the front of the house, and would then jump up and tip the bin over on one side to spill the contents. This meant easy access to any bits of leftover food. Usually the plan was foiled by Marble, who would send the fox off before the target was reached.

Then, there were the other cats: Ginge, a stringy ginger Tom who lived mid-road; Sleek, a new kid on the block who was black and white and thought he was pretty cool; Misty, a creamy Siamese she cat who lived opposite and was very spiteful, always spitting and complaining about something; and, finally, Korka, a brown and white cat who was quite elderly and only had one eye! His missing eye had been removed by the vet

after being damaged in a long
forgotten fight some years ago.

Ginge

sleek

Misty

KORKA

Sometimes Marble would keep the
neighbourhood awake with his late
night battles, which usually
involved lots of wailing, as he

defended his territory against the various competitors in the area.

Korka was very ferocious and never gave up. One night Marble battled for over two and a half hours with Korka before finally overcoming him.

The noise and general mayhem had been incredible: they were wailing, pouncing on each other, scratching and biting over and over again.

Eventually, the youthful strength of Marble decided the outcome, and as Korka tired, Marble sent him off with one last horrible bite on his hind leg. Korka went off howling and limping. Marble was exhausted, but happily the victor, and went back through the cat flap and home to his bed to lick his wounds. He has had a raggedy right ear ever since!

CHAPTER 5

THE CHRISTMAS TREE FIASCO

Christmas was always run according to family traditions for Ruby and Alex, and one of those concerned the tree: *always* a live Christmas tree was bought and then potted.

Next, it was decorated with an assortment of collected ornaments, beads and baubles. These were kept in a box in the attic and brought out each Christmas. As the collection had grown over the years, it had become a tradition to buy just one or two new ornaments each year- often something special- a particularly beautiful wooden or glass crafted decoration, (stars, angels and so on, being favoured).

Alongside these bought decorations were some which were decidedly 'home made' looking, (probably because they were). There were little velvet hearts that Ruby had stitched when she was in Infants; a paper blue and white star that Alex had made in nursery. But it was these touches that made the tree all the more special. And, added to this heady mix were the lights.

The tree went up, usually on Christmas Eve. Ruby and Alex both argued that some children at school had their tree up in early December, but Mum insisted that was too early.

This Christmas the tree had arrived, been potted, and they spent several hours decorating it; all the while arguing over which decoration should go where and with Mum surreptitiously repositioning a donkey, angel or star if it was felt to be in an 'unbalanced position'. When it was finished the last task was to switch on the lights. Alex was given that task, and they all agreed the tree looked wonderful.

Marble had been alongside during the entire operation. He had pulled bits of beading out of the box; flicked gold coins or sparkly stars across the room with a deft swing of his paw. He had at one point dived into the open decoration box, and ripping and tearing with his claws, he had shredded the tissue and newspaper inside, (which was used to cushion the decorations during storage), and attacked as if it was the enemy!

The tree was ready for Christmas. The task had been completed and in the morning the children would come down after opening their stockings, to find Father Christmas had deposited presents galore under the tree.

After everyone had gone to bed Marble, asleep on the bottom of Alex's bed, woke up. He was hungry, so decided to go looking for a midnight snack.

He jumped silently off the bed, poked his way through the gap in the doorway, out onto the landing. The house was very quiet-not a sound. He tip-toed across the landing and then down the stairs, avoiding the third step down that always creaked. Remembering the tree, he made his way to the sitting room and peered inside.

To his surprise the floor around the tree was covered: piled with presents, and he could smell something. His nose twitched...what was it? His curiosity was aroused: he had to find out what that smell was...He moved forward towards the tree, the smell was even stronger. 'Wow, what is that?' wondered Marble.

He could see lots of small presents, tied with glitter string, hanging from some of the lower branches of the tree; was the smell coming from there? He reached up. Some of the lower branches were quite sturdy. He might be able to climb up. He edged up onto a low branch where the smell was stronger, but it seemed to be coming from higher up. He poked his head upward and then placed his paws carefully onto a higher branch, and heaved. He managed to shove through the coarse knot of branches and spiked leaves and could see, just above his head, a small blue present with a gold label on it. It said MARBLE. Inside, (though Marble didn't yet know this), was a small cotton mouse stuffed with catnip. Now, cats love catnip, and this was what he could smell. He stretched his paw upwards, put his claws out and just managed to catch and tear the paper wrapping. The smell was even stronger. It sent Marble into a frenzy; he had to find out what was so enticing. With one last frantic push and swipe with his paw, he had the present in his grasp! 'Got it!' thought Marble.

But, as he reached up, his hind legs, which were balanced precariously on a thin branch below, kicked out behind and the branch snapped.

Marble tumbled, and as he tumbled his legs tangled in the beading which had been wound around the tree. His weight pulled the tree to one side. He thrashed around to try and hold on, but suddenly the tree wasn't just leaning to one side, it had started to fall! With an enormous smash the tree and decorations crashed to the floor! Marble wailed his loudest! 'What on earth had happened?' He tried to push his way out but his tail was pinned to the floor under a tree branch. There were broken ornaments, fragments of glass and shredded present wrappings everywhere. What a mess!

The mayhem had woken up the whole family. The noise had sounded as if Father Christmas and his crew of reindeer had just landed in the sitting room. They all came running down the stairs.

Mum threw her hands up in horror! "What? she asked."How could this happen?"

"Meow", said Marble.

Suddenly they all saw Marble buried among the mess.

"I knew that cat was trouble," laughed Dad.

Rather than be cross, they were so worried Marble had been hurt, all the children said was "Poor Marble!"

As the tree branches were lifted up Marble was put into Ruby's arms for a cuddle.

"I know," said Mum, "let's all have some hot chocolate, but first we'll clear up this mess."

"Can we open some presents then?" asked Alex.

"I don't see why not," said Dad.

"After all, it is Christmas," said Mum, and they all laughed.

CHAPTER 6

S.M.H. (Save My Hens)

Miss Lucy had been very anxious because a fox had been in her garden and had got to the eggs in the hen house. He had burrowed under the wire, somehow lifted the flaps giving access to the laying area, (where the eggs were), and had broken and eaten over a dozen eggs. A whole day's worth of laying!

Marble knew this because he had heard Miss Lucy talking to Pat next door.

"I don't know what to do," said Miss Lucy. "I'm worried the hens are not safe, but I have a proper hen house and run. It was supposed to be fox-proof; that's what the man said when I bought it. I just have to hope the fox doesn't return."

Marble made a mental note to keep an eye open and one ear on alert that night, to check if the fox had returned.

Later, asleep on Alex's bed, Marble heard a thud. It sounded like a piece of wood, or a stick, falling and hitting the ground. The bedroom window was slightly open. He listened carefully.

He padded silently over to the window and looked out. He could just catch sight of a corner of Miss Lucy's back garden, but only the edge of the hen house roof. He peered into the darkness, listening intently...he could see something, a dark shadow moving... It looked like a giant feather duster. It was moving across the rear hedge, silhouetted...and then it clicked! The rear light, Miss Lucy had just installed outside her kitchen window, was casting a shadow...the giant feather duster was the shadow of a bushy tail, a fox's tail!

Suddenly, Marble heard some murmuring from the hens; they had just been disturbed but were obviously not yet on full alarm. He must go, now!

Marble quickly scrambled out of the bedroom, down the stairs, (avoiding the third step that squeaked), and into the hallway and out through the cat flap.

The night air was cold. He had to go quietly down the narrow alley by Pat and Cedric's house, jump over the wall, across their garden and up onto the wall of Miss Lucy's garden. He was faster and more silent than Usain Bolt.

He could see the fox: he was full grown with a large bushy tail. The fox's tongue lolled out of his mouth and his teeth were dripping saliva, (he was obviously expecting a tasty chicken meal). The fox was now at the hen house fence. He started digging.

Marble dropped silently down on to the hen house roof. He stood still and pushed his chest out, pushed out his long claws, and then started to wail...louder than the ocean smashing onto rocks, blown by gale force winds; he wailed louder than a ship's foghorn...at the same time he

made all his hair stand on end. His
tail was like a spiky toilet brush

upright in the air, and his body
was twice its normal size. He
looked like a giant furry Brillo pad

with lamp like green eyes. He looked and sounded like a huge monster.

"Whooo MEOW, whaaa..." On and on he screamed and wailed.

The fox froze and looked up.

The hens were now all awake and going frantic; hysterically clucking and scratching around.

What WAS that noise? It sounded like a banshee. This was definitely NOT good news decided the fox. He caught sight of Marble's profile silhouetted against the night sky. What was it? It looked and sounded terrifying.

It was so loud bedroom windows started to open: the neighbours had been woken up. "What is *that noise*?" people screamed.

"Pipe down I've got to get to work tomorrow"

"Shut that darn cat up," said one.

"Who is that?" said Pat and Cedric.

Ruby and Alex had both woken up and ran into their parents' room afraid. "What is it?" they asked.

"My hens," said Miss Lucy.

Marble suddenly dived at the fox. He went straight for his face, biting and scrabbling furiously with his feet, claws extended, ripping and tearing. "Howl, howl" yelled the fox. He tried to shake Marble off, but still he clung on with his long claws digging into the fox's flesh. The fox shuddered. He stood still and then made an enormous effort to dislodge Marble. The scraggy red fox did a weird corkscrew movement with his body, and then shook his head so violently that Marble thought he might be catapulted all the way to the moon.

Marble crashed to the floor.

All the accompanying noise from the hens, the neighbours and this 'demon', (or whatever it was), had petrified the fox, and he turned and ran; scrambling over the garden wall, into the road behind, and off towards Cricklewood.

Marble stood up, took a deep breath, flattened down most of his fur, licked a bit that persisted in sticking out and glued it down with his saliva. He then calmly went back home: over the side wall, across Pat and Cedric's garden and over their wall, up the alley, back through the cat flap and back to Alex's bed.

"Thank goodness you're back Marble," said Alex. "There was something going on outside tonight."

'Yes, I know', thought Marble.

And they both curled up and went to sleep. Outside all was now quiet.

The next day, sitting in his usual position by the garden gate, Marble was hailed a hero.

"Was that you making that incredible sound last night? asked the Rock Star. "Hear you saved Miss Lucy's hens."

"Well done", said Pat and Cedric. "You were very brave Marble."

"Thank you," said Miss Lucy. "My poor hens would have been that fox's supper, if not for you. You are a hero Marble, you saved my hens!"

When Ruby and Alex heard what Marble had done they made him a medal out of gold card and strung it onto his little collar. They were very proud, and so was Marble.

CHAPTER 7

CATNAPPED

There was a grumpy man called Mr Johnjo who lived in a road around the corner from the Greek Roads. He thought Marble was spoiling his vegetable patch by peeing on the plants!

He saw Ruby on West End Lane coming from the shops: "I won't have it," he said. "Your pesky cat is using my vegetable patch as a toilet. It is killing my cabbages, and I won't have it!"

"Sorry," said Ruby. "We'll try to keep him at home."

Mr Johnjo didn't much like animals, 'dirty creatures' he called them. If he saw That Cat in his garden again he was going to do something about it! Yes, he was going to DO SOMETHING ABOUT IT!

It is true that Marble did sometimes go into Mr Johnjo's garden, but not to use it as a toilet, (he had his litter tray at home for that), but because there was a small patch of particularly soft, springy grass that just caught the sunshine at about noon each day. He could happily snooze in the warm sun and occasionally give chase after one of the many birds that frequented the garden in search of the very juicy worms in the vegetable patch!

One day, Marble got up, and after a delicious breakfast of kippers, wandered around the kitchen and through the hall. There appeared to be a lot of packing cases and boxes piled up. Mum seemed stressed and was asking Ruby and Alex to finish up their breakfast "Quickly, because there is *so* much to do." Marble didn't give it much thought and went outside through the cat flap to sit on Sentry duty by the garden gate. A few weeks before he had noticed a big sign had been put up in the front garden, and this was blocking out the sun from shining on the exact spot where he sat.

So, it was on this day, as the full sun glowed down, around 12noon, that Marble went off to find his comfy snooze patch in Mr Johnjo's garden.

What he didn't know was that the day before, Korka had been in Mr Johnjo's garden and had dug up some carrots as he had nosed around the vegetable patch. He had also sat his very ample bottom down, (splat!), on some tomato plants...and the tomatoes had gone, well—SPLAT!! They looked more like the tomato puree that Dad buys for spaghetti bolognaise sauce, (you know the red mush you buy in tubes at the supermarket). Anyway, Mr Johnjo was not a happy man.

"That pesky cat! I'm going to teach him a lesson!" he threatened.

Mr Johnjo had a plan; a plan Marble had absolutely no idea about as he lay snoozing on his favourite patch of soft, springy grass...he was dreaming of fish for supper, perhaps some tender, white cod, and he was about to lick his lips when WHACK! Some sort of net had crashed down over him! The metal frame had caught his tail and a sharp stab of pain shot through his body. He jumped up with a wail.

Mr Johnjo shouted triumphantly: "Got you!"

As Marble had leapt into the air he had simply pulled the netting upwards with him and Mr Johnjo had skilfully twisted the handle on the frame so the net had twisted back on itself, and had sealed Marble in! There was no escape! The more he struggled the more tangled he became. "Meow! Meow! Meow!" wailed Marble.

"That'll teach you," said Mr Johnjo as he carried his struggling cargo down the path to his garden shed. When inside he pulled the netting apart and released Marble, but there was nowhere to run!

"You'll stay in there", said Mr Johnjo, "until you and that girl Ruby learn your lesson!"

Then he slammed the door.

Marble looked around. It was very dark, and the small window was very grimy so didn't let in much light, but the door was locked and there was no way out!

Mr Johnjo kept Marble locked in the shed on his own for days. He would occasionally give him an open tin of cat food and some water to drink, but Marble nearly cut his tongue on the sharp metal edges of the can lid, and the water soon went stale. Some litter had been put in a cardboard box, but it became very smelly because Mr Johnjo didn't bother to clean it out.

What Marble didn't know was that while he was locked up, Ruby, Alex, Mum and Dad were preparing to move house. They were leaving London to go and live in the country.

Marble was lonely, frightened and desperate to get home. Of course, as time passed, he didn't know that now there was no home to go to.

Meanwhile, Ruby, Alex, and Mum and Dad were staying in a hotel in the Cotswolds, while they waited for their new home to be ready. All of their toys and furniture had gone into storage. And, as for Marble, well they didn't know what had happened...he had gone missing days before the new owners of their house were moving in. Ruby and Alex had cried and cried...

"He'll probably go back to the house," said Mum. "We'll keep in touch with the new owners. He'll turn up."

But he didn't, and several weeks went by.

Mum had already alerted Mr Arkwright, the vet who had looked after Marble since he was a kitten. With help from a tearful Ruby and Alex, Mum had put up cards in the surgery, and all around the Neighbourhood.

THEN, a neighbour heard Mr Johnjo boasting about how he had captured Marble, and locked him up, to 'teach that family a lesson'.

Mum told Mr Arkwright.

He rang Mr Johnjo and told him, "You either bring that cat to my surgery by 6p.m. this evening, or I'll call the police."

At 6.30p.m. Mr Arkwright called to say he had Marble safe.

It was several months before the family moved into their new home. Meanwhile Mr Arkwright kept Marble safely at his surgery. He would often sit observing in the surgery and settled in surprisingly well considering Mr Arkwright's dog had free run of the place. But Marble had accepted the little Jack Russell, (perhaps because he had invaded the dog's space, rather than the other way around?). Mr Arkwright said Marble was an extremely intelligent cat, interested in all going on around him and would watch as he dealt with his patients, whether they were dogs, cats or hamsters! Ruby and Alex were allowed to make visits to Marble, but were thrilled when they were able to collect him to transport him to their new home in the country.

The new house was much larger than the London house, with a front and back garden, double gates and a high wall all around. There was a lawn to play on, a vegetable patch, flowers and a patio. Inside there was room for the children to have a large playroom as well as their own bedrooms.

Marble was now creeping towards old age. Alex cuddled his soft fur

as they took him out of his cat
carrier.

"Marble," said Ruby and Alex,
"This is your retirement home."

Alex placed Marble gently down.

"Well, I don't know about that,"
said Marble to himself. "I can smell
all kinds of exciting new scents,
and yes, I'm sure I can smell mice!
Don't think I'll be retiring just yet.
There's still a job to do."

And with that he ran off to explore.

HOW TO CALCULATE YOUR CAT'S AGE.

When your cat is 2 years old he is like a 25 year old human! For every year your cat lives after that you add 4 years. So...

CAT YEARS	HUMAN YEARS
2	25
3	29
4	33
5	37
6	41
7	45
8	49
9	53
10	57